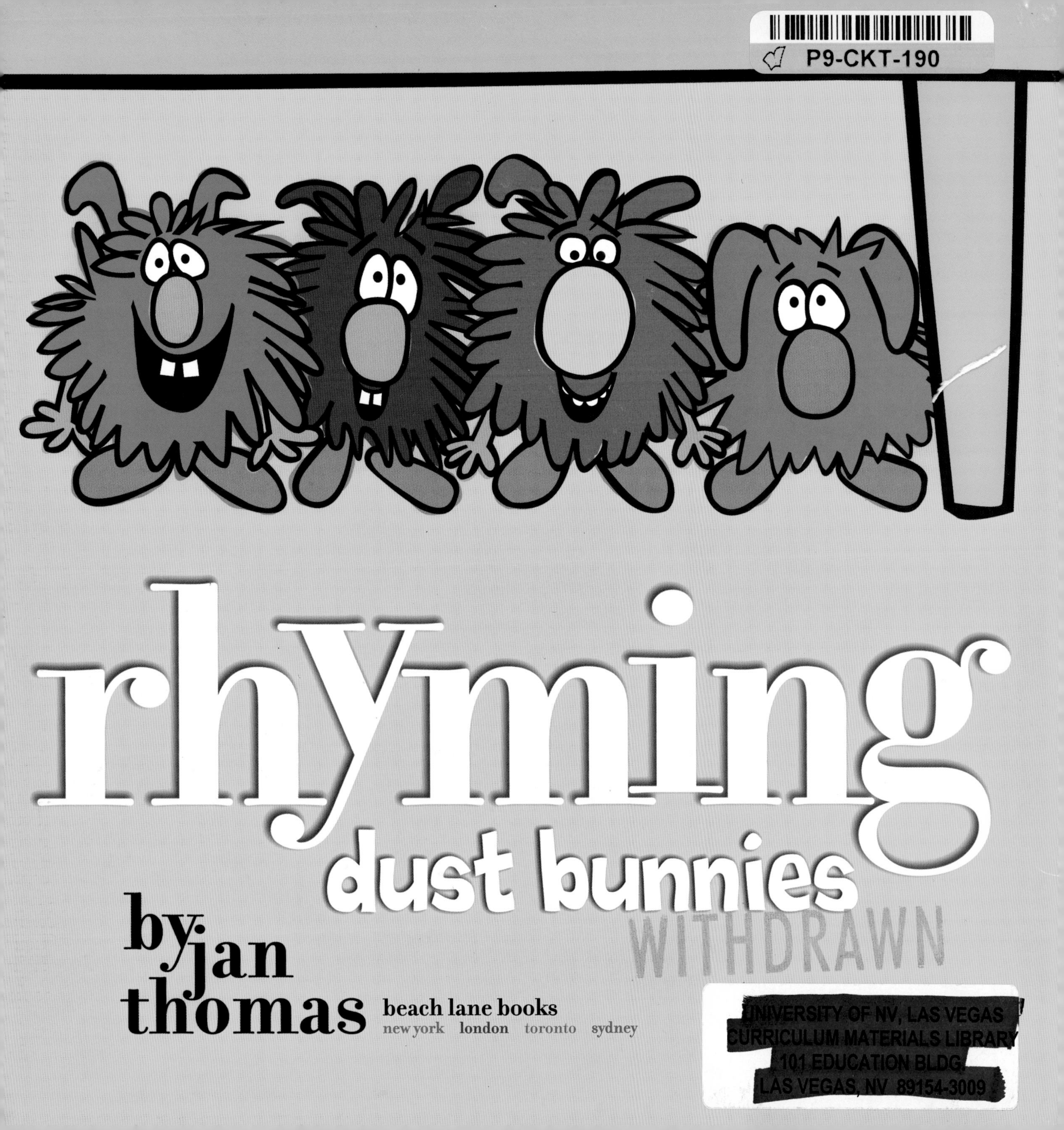
rhyming dust bunnies
by jan thomas
beach lane books
new york london toronto sydney

Hello! We are
Ed, Ned, Ted . . .
and Bob.
We rhyme

all the time!

tar
LOOK!

No, Bob . . . "**LOOK!**"
does not rhyme with **car**!

What rhymes with bug?

hug
rug

mug
LOOK OUT!

No, Bob . . . "**LOOK OUT!**"
does not rhyme with **bug!**

What rhymes with dog?

hog
log
fog

LOOK OUT!
HERE COMES A BIG
SCARY MONSTER
WITH A BROOM!

Bob, no . . . "**LOOK OUT! HERE COMES A BIG SCARY MONSTER WITH A BROOM!**"

does not rhyme with **ANYTHING**, really.

Okay then, but . . .

RUN

FOR IT!

AHHH!!

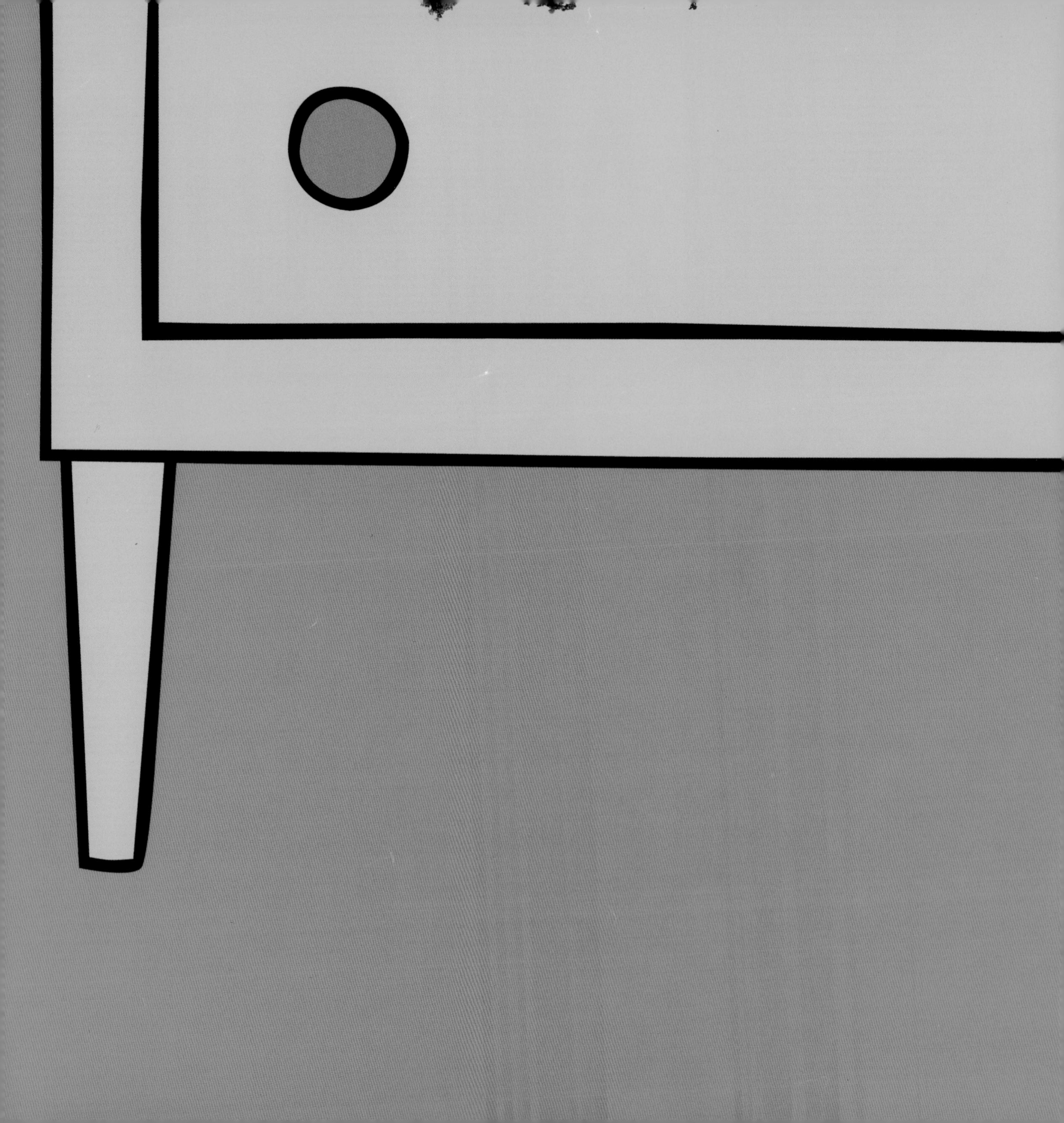

Good call, Bob.

Okay, so where were we?
What rhymes with **cat**?

sat
pat

rat

Thwptt

Um, Bob,
what rhymes with
HOW DO WE GET OUT?

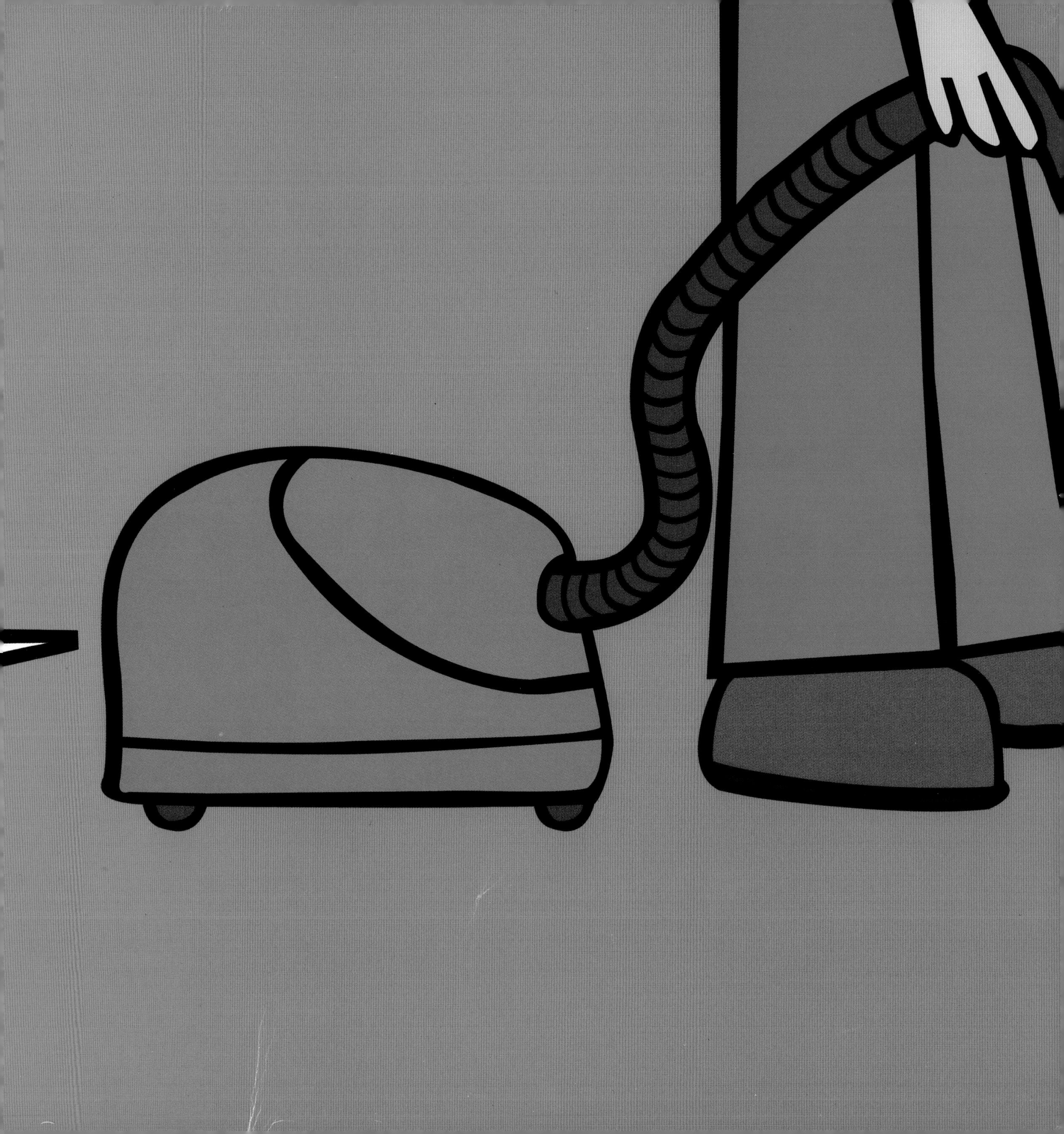

Beach Lane Books
An imprint of Simon & Schuster Children's
Publishing Division
1230 Avenue of the Americas
New York, New York 10020

Book design by Jan Thomas and Ann Bobco
The text for this book is set in Filosofia and Eatwell.
The illustrations for this book are rendered digitally.
Manufactured in China
10 9 8 7 6 5 4 3 2
Library of Congress Cataloging-in-Publication Data
Thomas, Jan, 1958–
Rhyming dust bunnies / [text and illustrations by]
Jan Thomas. — 1st ed.
p. cm.
Summary: As three dust bunnies, Ed, Ned, and Ted, are
demonstrating how much they love to rhyme, a fourth,
Bob, is trying to warn them of approaching danger.
ISBN-13: 978-1-4169-7976-0 (alk. paper)
ISBN-10: 1-4169-7976-X (alk. paper)
[1. Rhyme—Fiction. 2. Dust—Fiction.
3. Humorous stories.] I. Title.
PZ7.T36694Rhy 2008
[E]—dc22
2008028779

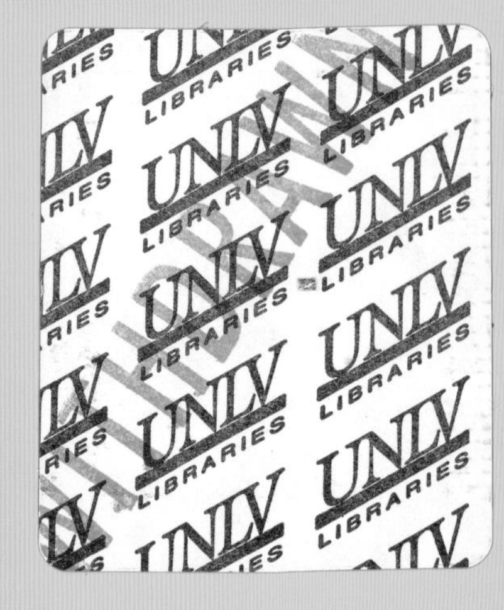